Henry Fitz Randolph

**Under the Holly**

Christmas-Tide in Song and Story

Henry Fitz Randolph

**Under the Holly**
*Christmas-Tide in Song and Story*

ISBN/EAN: 9783743386303

Manufactured in Europe, USA, Canada, Australia, Japa

Cover: Foto ©Andreas Hilbeck / pixelio.de

Manufactured and distributed by brebook publishing software
(www.brebook.com)

Henry Fitz Randolph

**Under the Holly**

# Christmas-Tide

IN

# SONG AND STORY.

\* \*

NEW YORK:

ANSON D. F. RANDOLPH AND COMPANY,

38 WEST TWENTY-THIRD STREET.

University Press:
John Wilson and Son, Cambridge.

# CONTENTS.

———◆———

Now that the time is come wherein
　　Our Saviour Christ was born,
The larders full of beef and pork,
　　The garners filled with corn;
As God hath plenty to thee sent,
　　Take comfort of thy labors,
And let it never thee repent
　　To feast thy needy neighbors.

*The winter thorn*
*Blossoms at Christmas, mindful of our Lord.*

*Some say that ever 'gainst that season comes*
*Wherein our Saviour's birth is celebrated,*
*This bird of dawning singeth all night long:*
*And then, they say, no spirit dares stir abroad;*
*The nights are wholesome, -- then no planets strike,*
*No fairy takes, no witch hath power to charm,*
*So hallowed and so gracious is the time.*

*It was always said of him, that he knew how to keep*
*Christmas well, if any man alive possessed the knowledge.*
*May that be truly said of us, and all of us! And so, as*
*Tiny Tim observed, God bless Us, Every One !*

*At Christmas play and make good cheer*
*For Christmas comes but once a year.*

*Extract from "The Sketch Book"*
*of Washington Irving.*

## CHRISTMAS.

O F all the old festivals, that of Christmas awakens the strongest and most heartfelt associations. There is a tone of solemn and sacred feeling that blends with our conviviality, and lifts the spirit to a state of hallowed and elevated enjoyment. The services of the church about this season are extremely tender and inspiring. They dwell on the beautiful story of the origin of our faith, and the pastoral scenes that accompanied its announcement. They gradually increase in fervor and pathos during the season of Advent, until they break forth in full jubilee on the morning that brought peace and good-will to men. I do not know a grander effect of music on the moral feelings than to hear the full choir and the pealing organ performing a Christmas anthem in a cathedral, and filling every part of the vast pile with triumphant harmony.

It is a beautiful arrangement, also, derived
from days of yore, that this festival, which com-
memorates the announcement of the religion of
peace and love, has been made the season for
gathering together of family connections, and
drawing closer again those bands of kindred
hearts which the cares and pleasures and sorrows
of the world are continually operating to cast
loose ; of calling back the children of a family
who have launched forth in life, and wandered
widely asunder, once more to assemble about
the paternal hearth, that rallying-place of the
affections, there to grow young and loving again
among the endearing mementos of childhood.

There is something in the very season of the
year that gives a charm to the festivity of Christmas.    At other times we derive a great portion of
our pleasures from the mere beauties of Nature.
Our feelings sally forth and dissipate themselves
over the sunny landscape, and we "live abroad
and everywhere."  The song of the bird, the
murmur of the stream, the breathing fragrance
of spring, the soft voluptuousness of summer, the
golden pomp of autumn ; earth with its mantle
of refreshing green, and heaven with its deep
delicious blue and its cloudy magnificence, — all
fill us with mute but exquisite delight, and we

revel in the luxury of mere sensation. But in the depth of winter, when Nature lies despoiled of every charm, and wrapped in her shroud of sheeted snow, we turn for our gratifications to moral sources. The dreariness and desolation of the landscape, the short gloomy days and darksome nights, while they circumscribe our wanderings, shut in our feelings also from rambling abroad, and make us more keenly disposed for the pleasures of the social circle. Our thoughts are more concentrated; our friendly sympathies more aroused. We feel more sensibly the charm of each other's society, and are brought more closely together by dependence on each other for enjoyment. Heart calleth unto heart; and we draw our pleasures from the deep wells of living kindness, which lie in the quiet recesses of our bosoms, and which, when resorted to, furnish forth the pure element of domestic felicity.

The pitchy gloom without makes the heart dilate on entering the room filled with the glow and warmth of the evening fire. The ruddy blaze diffuses an artificial summer and sunshine through the room, and lights up each countenance into a kindlier welcome. Where does the honest face of hospitality expand into a broader

and more cordial smile, where is the shy glance
of love more sweetly eloquent, than by the winter fireside? and as the hollow blast of wintry
wind rushes through the hall, claps the distant
door, whistles about the casement, and rumbles
down the chimney, what can be more grateful
than that feeling of sober and sheltered security
with which we look round upon the comfortable
chamber and the scene of domestic hilarity?

The English, from the great prevalence of
rural habits throughout every class of society,
have always been fond of those festivals and
holidays which agreeably interrupt the stillness
of country life; and they were, in former days,
particularly observant of the religious and social
rites of Christmas. It is inspiring to read even
the dry details which some antiquarians have
given of the quaint humors, the burlesque pa-
geants, the complete abandonment to mirth and
good-fellowship, with which this festival was celebrated. It seemed to throw open every door,
and unlock every heart. It brought the peasant
and the peer together, and blended all ranks in
one warm, generous flow of joy and kindness.
The old halls of castles and manor-houses resounded with the harp and the Christmas carol,
and their ample boards groaned under the weight

of hospitality. Even the poorest cottage welcomed the festive season with green decorations of bay and holly; the cheerful fire glanced its rays through the lattice, inviting the passenger to raise the latch, and join the gossip knot huddled round the hearth, beguiling the long evening with legendary jokes and oft-told Christmas tales.

One of the least pleasing effects of modern refinement is the havoc it has made among the hearty old holiday customs. It has completely taken off the sharp touchings and spirited reliefs of these embellishments of life, and has worn down society into a more smooth and polished, but certainly a less characteristic surface. Many of the games and ceremonials of Christmas have entirely disappeared, and like the sherris-sack of old Falstaff, are become matters of speculation and dispute among commentators. They flourished in times full of spirit and lustihood, when men enjoyed life roughly, but heartily and vigorously, — times wild and picturesque, which have furnished poetry with its richest materials, and the drama with its most attractive variety of characters and manners. The world has become more worldly. There is more of dissipation and less of enjoyment. Pleasure has expanded into a broader but a shallower stream, and has forsaken many of those deep and quiet channels where it flowed sweetly through the calm bosom of domestic life. Society has acquired a more enlightened and elegant tone; but it has lost many of its strong local peculiarities, its home-bred feelings, its honest fireside delights. The traditionary customs of golden-hearted antiquity, its feudal hospitalities and lordly wassailings, have passed away with the baronial castles and stately manor-houses in which they were celebrated. They comported with the shadowy hall, the great oaken gallery, and the tapestried parlor, but are unfitted to the light showy saloons and gay drawing-rooms of the modern villa.

Shorn, however, as it is, of its ancient and festive honors, Christmas is still a period of delightful excitement in England. It is gratifying to see that home feeling completely aroused which seems to hold so powerful a place in every English bosom. The preparations making on every side for the social board that is again to unite friends and kindred; the presents of good cheer passing and repassing, those tokens of regard and quickeners of kind feelings; the evergreens distributed about houses and churches, emblems of peace and gladness, — all these have the most pleasing effect in producing fond associations, and kindling benevolent sympathies. Even the sound of the waits, rude as may be their minstrelsy, breaks upon the mid-watches of a winter night with the effect of perfect harmony. As I have been awakened by them in that still and solemn hour, "when deep sleep falleth upon man," I have listened with a hushed delight, and, connecting them with the sacred and joyous occasion, have almost fancied them into another celestial choir, announcing peace and good-will to mankind.

. . . . . . . . .

Amidst the general call to happiness, the bustle of the spirits, and stir of the affections, which prevail at this period, what bosom can remain insensible? It is, indeed, the season of regenerated feeling, — the season for kindling, not merely the fire of hospitality in the hall, but the genial flame of charity in the heart.

The scene of early love again rises green to memory beyond the sterile waste of years ; and the idea of home, fraught with the fragrance of home-dwelling joys, re-animates the drooping spirit, — as the Arabian breeze will sometimes waft the freshness of the distant fields to the weary pilgrim of the desert.

. . . . . . . . .

He who can turn churlishly away from con-
templating the felicity of his fellow-beings, and
sit down darkling and repining in his loneliness
when all around is joyful, may have his moments
of strong excitement and selfish gratification, but
he wants the genial and social sympathies which
constitute the charm of a merry Christmas.

*Dedication of Wordsworth's River Duddon Sonnets,
to his brother Dr. Wordsworth.*

## CHRISTMAS MINSTRELSY.

THE minstrels played their Christmas tune
    To-night beneath my cottage eaves ;
While smitten by a lofty moon,
    The encircling laurels, thick with leaves,
Gave back a rich and dazzling sheen,
That overpowered their natural green.

Through hill and valley every breeze
    Had sunk to rest with folded wings :
Keen was the air, but could not freeze
    Nor check the music of the strings ;
So stout and hardy were the band
That scraped the chords with strenuous hand.

And who but listened ? — till was paid
    Respect to every inmate's claim :
The greeting given, the music played,
    In honor of each household name,
Duly pronounced with lusty call,
And a merry Christmas wished to all.

2

O Brother! I revere the choice
   That took thee from thy native hills;
And it is given thee to rejoice :
   Though public care full often tills
(Heaven only witness of the toil)
A barren and ungrateful soil.

Yet would that thou, with me and mine,
   Hadst heard this never-failing rite;
And seen on other faces shine
   A true revival of the light
Which Nature and these rustic powers,
In simple childhood, spread through ours !

For pleasure hath not ceased to wait
   On these expected annual rounds,
Whether the rich man's sumptuous gate
   Call forth the unelaborate sounds,
Or they are offered at the door
That guards the lowliest of the poor.

How touching, when at midnight sweep
   Snow-muffled winds, and all is dark,
To hear — and sink again to sleep !
   Or at an earlier call, to mark,
By blazing fire, the still suspense
Of self-complacent innocence;

The mutual nod, — the grave disguise
  Of hearts with gladness brimming o'er,
And some unbidden tears that rise
  For names once heard, and heard no more ;
Tears brightened by the serenade
For infant in the cradle laid !

Ah ! not for emerald fields alone,
  With ambient streams more pure and bright
Than fabled Cytherea's zone
  Glittering before the Thunderer's sight,
Is to my heart of hearts endeared
The ground where we were born and reared !

Hail ancient manners ! sure defence,
  Where they survive, of wholesome laws ;
Remnants of love whose modest sense
  Thus into narrow room withdraws :
Hail usages of pristine mould,
And ye that guard them, mountains old !

Bear with me, Brother ! quench the thought
  That slights this passion or condemns ;
If thee fond fancy ever brought
  From the proud margin of the Thames,
And Lambeth's venerable towers,
To humbler streams and greener bowers.

Yes, they can make, who fail to find,
   Short leisure even in busiest days;
Moments to cast a look behind,
   And profit by those kindly rays
That through the clouds do sometimes steal,
And all the far-off past reveal.

Hence, while the imperial city's din
   Beats frequent on thy satiate ear,
A pleased attention I may win
   To agitations less severe,
That neither overwhelm nor cloy,
But fill the hollow vale with joy!

*By John Addington Symonds.*

## A CHRISTMAS LULLABY.

SLEEP, baby, sleep ! the Mother sings :
  Heaven's angels kneel and fold their wings :
      Sleep, baby, sleep !

With swathes of scented hay thy bed
By Mary's hand at eve was spread.
      Sleep, baby, sleep !

At midnight came the shepherds, they
Whom seraphs wakened by the way.
      Sleep, baby, sleep !

And three kings from the East afar
Ere dawn came guided by thy star.
      Sleep, baby, sleep !

They brought thee gifts of gold and gems,
Pure orient pearls, rich diadems.
      Sleep, baby, sleep !

But thou who liest slumbering there,
Art King of kings, earth, ocean, air.
　　　Sleep, baby, sleep!

Sleep, baby, sleep!　The shepherds sing;
Through heaven, through earth, hosannas ring.
　　　Sleep, baby, sleep!

*By Hans Christian Andersen.*

## THE OLD OAK-TREE'S LAST DREAM.

THE Oak-tree stood stripped of all his foliage, ready to go to rest for the whole winter, and in it to dream many dreams, — to dream of the past, just as men dream.

The tree had once been a little one, and had had a field for its cradle. Now, according to human reckoning, he was in his fourth century. He was the tallest and mightiest tree in the woods; his crown towered high above all the other trees, and was seen far out on the sea, serving as a beacon to ships; but the old Oak-tree had never thought how many eyes sought him out from afar.

High up in his green crown wood-doves had built their nests, and the cuckoo perched to announce spring; and in the autumn, when his leaves looked like copper-plates hammered out thin, birds of passage came and rested awhile

among the boughs, before they flew across the
seas. But now it was winter; the tree stood
leafless, and the bowed and crooked branches
displayed their dark outlines; crows and jack-
daws came alternately, gossiping together about
the hard times that were beginning, and the
difficulty of getting food during the winter.

It was just at the holy Christmas-tide that the
Oak-tree dreamt his most beautiful dream : this
dream we will hear.

The tree had a foreboding that a festive season
was nigh ; he seemed to hear the church-bells
ringing all round, and to feel as though it were a
mild, warm summer day. Fresh and green, he
reared his mighty crown on high ; the sunbeams
played among his leaves and boughs ; the air was
filled with fragrance ; bright-colored butterflies
gambolled, and gnats danced, — which was all
they could do to show their joy. And all that
the tree had beheld during his life passed by as
in a festive procession. Knights and ladies, with
feathers in their caps, and hawks perching on
their wrists, rode gayly through the wood ; dogs
barked, and the huntsman sounded his bugle.
Then came foreign soldiers in bright armor and
gay vestments, bearing spears and halberds, setting up their tents, and presently taking them

down again; then watch-fires blazed up, and
bands of wild outlaws sang, revelled, and slept
under the tree's outstretched boughs, or happy
lovers met in the quiet moonlight, and carved
their initials on the grayish bark. At one time
a guitar, at another an Æolian harp, had been
hung up amid the old oak's boughs, by merry
travelling apprentices; now they hung there
again, and the wind played so sweetly with the
strings. The wood-doves cooed, as though they
would do their best to express the tree's happy
feelings, and the cuckoo talked about himself as
usual, proclaiming how many summer days he
had to live.

And now it seemed a new and stronger current
of life flowed through him, down to his lowest
roots, up to his highest twigs, even to the very
leaves! The tree felt in his roots that a warm life
stirred in the earth, — felt his strength increase, and
that he was growing taller and taller. His trunk
shot up more and more; his crown grew fuller;
he spread, he towered; and still, as the tree grew,
he felt that his power grew with it, and that his
ardent longing to advance higher and higher up
to the bright warm sun increased also.

Already had he towered above the clouds,
which drifted below him, now like a troop of

dark-plumaged birds of passage, now like flocks of large white swans.

And every leaf could see, as though it had eyes; the stars became visible by daylight, so large and bright, each one sparkling like a mild, clear eye : they reminded him of dear kind eyes that had sought each other under his shade, — lovers' eyes, children's eyes.

It was a blessed moment; and yet, in the height of his joy, the Oak-tree felt a desire and longing that all the other trees, bushes, herbs, and flowers of the wood might be lifted up with him, might share in this glory and gladness. The mighty Oak-tree, amid his dream of splendor, could not be fully blessed unless he might have all, little and great, to share it with him; and this feeling thrilled through boughs and leaves as strongly, as fervently as though his were the heart of a man.

The tree's crown bowed itself, as though it missed and sought something, looked backward. Then he felt the fragrance of honeysuckles and violets, and fancied he could hear the cuckoo answering himself.

Yes, so it was! for now peeped forth, through the clouds, the green summits of the wood; the other trees below had grown and lifted themselves up likewise ; bushes and herbs shot high into the air, some tearing themselves loose from their roots, and mounting all the faster. The birch had grown most rapidly ; like a flash of white lightning, its slender stem shot upward, its boughs waving like pale-green banners. Even the feathery brown reed had pierced its way through the clouds ; and the birds followed, and sang and sang; and on the grass that fluttered to and fro like a long streaming green ribbon perched the grasshopper, and drummed with his wings on his lean body ; the cockchafers hummed, and the bees buzzed ; every bird sang with all his might, and all was music and gladness.

"But the little blue flower near the water, — I want that too," said the Oak-tree ; "and the bell-flower, and the dear little daisy ! " The tree wanted all these.

"We are here ! we are here ! " chanted sweet low voices on all sides.

"But the pretty anemones of last spring, and the bed of lilies-of-the-valley that blossomed the year before that ! and the wild crab-apple tree ! and all the beautiful trees and flowers that have adorned the wood through so many seasons — oh, would that they had lived till now ! "

"We are here! we are here!" was the answer; and this time it seemed to come from the air above, as though they had fled upward first.

"Oh, this is too great happiness, — it is almost incredible!" exclaimed the Oak-tree. "I have them all, small and great; not one of them is forgotten! How can such blessedness be possible?"

"In the kingdom of God all things are possible," was the answer.

And the tree now felt that his roots were loosening themselves from the earth. "This is best of all," he said; "now no bonds shall detain me, I can soar up to the height of light and glory; and my dear ones are with me, small and great, — I have them all!"

. . . . . . . . .

Such was the old Oak-tree's dream; and all the while, on that holy Christmas Eve, a mighty storm swept over sea and land: the ocean rolled its heavy billows on the shore; the tree cracked, was rent and torn up by the roots, at the very moment when he dreamt that his roots were disengaging themselves from the earth. He fell. His three hundred and sixty-five years were now as a day is to the May-fly.

On Christmas morning, when the sun burst

forth, the storm was laid. All the church-bells were ringing joyously ; and from every chimney, even the poorest, the blue smoke curled upward, as from the Druids' altar of old uprose the sacrificial steam. The sea was calm again ; and a large vessel that had weathered the storm the night before, now hoisted all its flags, in token of Yule festivity. "The tree is gone, — the old Oak-tree, our beacon," said the crew; "it has fallen during last night's storm. How can its place ever be supplied?"

This was the tree's funeral eulogium, brief but well-meant. There he lay, outstretched upon the snowy carpet near the shore ; whilst over it re-echoed the hymn sung on shipboard, — the hymn sung in thanksgiving for the joy of Christmas, for the bliss of the human soul's salvation, through Christ, and the gift of eternal life : —-

"Sing loud, and raise your voices high,
  For your redemption draweth nigh ;
  Lift up your heads, and have no fear !
  The promised kingdom, it is here !
  Oh, take the gift, in joy receive ;
  All things are his who will believe :
  O little flock, what words can tell
  The bliss of souls Christ loved so well ?
          Hallelujah ! Hallelujah !"

Thus resounded the old hymn ; and every soul lifted up heart and desire heavenward, even as the old tree had lifted himself on his last, best dream, — his Christmas Eve dream.

## LITTLE GOTTLIEB.

A CROSS the German Ocean,
  In a country far from our own,
Once, a poor little boy, named Gottlieb,
  Lived with his mother alone.

They dwelt in a part of the village
  Where the houses were poor and small,
But the house of little Gottlieb
  Was the poorest one of all.

He was not large enough to work,
  And his mother could no more
(Though she scarcely laid her knitting down)
  Than keep the wolf from the door.

She had to take their threadbare clothes,
  And turn, and patch, and darn ;
For never any woman yet
  Grew rich by knitting yarn.

And oft at night beside her chair
    Would Gottlieb sit, and plan
The wonderful things he would do for her
    When he grew to be a man.

One night she sat and knitted,
    And Gottlieb sat and dreamed,
When a happy fancy all at once
    Upon his vision beamed.

'T was only a week till Christmas,
    And Gottlieb knew that then
The Christ-child, who was born that day,
    Sent down good gifts to men.

But he said, " He will never find us,
    Our home is so mean and small ;
And we, who have most need of them,
    Will get no gifts at all."

When all at once a happy light
    Came into his eyes so blue,
And lighted up his face with smiles,
    As he thought what he could do.

Next day, when the postman's letters
    Came from all over the land,

Came one for the Christ-child, written
In a child's poor, trembling hand.

You may think he was sorely puzzled
What in the world to do ;
So he went to the Burgomaster,
As the wisest man he knew.

And when they opened the letter,
They stood almost dismayed,
That such a little child should dare
To ask the Lord for aid.

Then the Burgomaster stammered,
And scarce knew what to speak,
And hastily he brushed aside
A drop, like a tear, from his cheek.

Then up he spoke right gruffly,
And turned himself about :
" This must be a very foolish boy,
And a small one, too, no doubt."

But when six rosy children
That night about him pressed,
Poor, trusting little Gottlieb
Stood near him, with the rest.

3

And he heard his simple, touching prayer
  Through all their noisy play,
Though he tried his very best to put
  The thought of him away.

A wise and learned man was he,
  Men called him good and just ;
But his wisdom seemed like foolishness,
  By that weak child's simple trust.

Now, when the morn of Christmas came,
  And the long, long week was done,
Poor Gottlieb, who scarce could sleep,
  Rose up before the sun,

And hastened to his mother ;
  But he scarce might speak for fear,
When he saw her wondering look, and saw
  The Burgomaster near.

He was n't afraid of the Holy Babe,
  Nor his mother, meek and mild ;
But he felt as if so great a man
  Had never been a child.

Amazed the poor child looked, to find
  The hearth was piled with wood,

And the table, never full before,
  Was heaped with dainty food.

Then, half to hide from himself the truth,
  The Burgomaster said,
While the mother blessed him on her knees,
  And Gottlieb shook for dread :

"Nay, give no thanks, my good dame,
  To such as me for aid ;
Be grateful to your little son,
  And the Lord, to whom he prayed !"

Then turning round to Gottlieb,
  "Your written prayer, you see,
Came not to whom it was addressed,
  It only came to me !

"'T was but a foolish thing you did,
  As you must understand ;
For though the gifts are yours, you know,
  You have them from my hand."

Then Gottlieb answered fearlessly,
  Where he humbly stood apart,
"But the Christ-child sent them all the same ;
  He put the thought in your heart !"

## TINY TIM'S CHRISTMAS DINNER.

THEN up rose Mrs. Cratchit, Cratchit's wife, dressed out but poorly in a twice turned gown, but brave in ribbons, which are cheap and make a goodly show for sixpence; and she laid the cloth, assisted by Belinda Cratchit, second of her daughters, also brave in ribbons; while Master Peter Cratchit plunged a fork into the saucepan of potatoes, and getting the corners of his monstrous shirt-collar (Bob's private property, conferred upon his son and heir in honor of the day) into his mouth, rejoiced to find himself so gallantly attired, and yearned to show his linen in the fashionable Parks. And now two smaller Cratchits, boy and girl, came tearing in, screaming that outside the baker's they had smelt the goose, and known it for their own; and basking in luxurious thoughts of sage and onion, these young Cratchits danced about the table, and exalted Master Peter Cratchit to the skies,

while he (not proud, although his collars nearly
choked him) blew the fire, until the slow potatoes,
bubbling up, knocked loudly at the saucepan
lid to be let out and peeled.

"What has ever got your precious father
then?" said Mrs. Cratchit. "And your brother
Tiny Tim! And Martha warn't as late last
Christmas Day by half an hour!"

"Here's Martha, mother!" said a girl, ap-
pearing as she spoke.

"Here's Martha, mother!" cried the two
young Cratchits. "Hurrah! There's *such* a
goose, Martha!"

"Why, bless your heart alive, my dear, how
late you are!" said Mrs. Cratchit, kissing her a
dozen times, and taking off her shawl and bonnet
for her with officious zeal.

"We'd a deal of work to finish up last night,"
replied the girl, "and had to clear away this
morning, mother!"

"Well! never mind so long as you are come,"
said Mrs. Cratchit. "Sit ye down before the fire,
my dear, and have a warm, Lord bless ye!"

"No, no! there's father coming," cried the
two young Cratchits, who were everywhere at
once. "Hide, Martha, hide!"

So Martha hid herself; and in came little Bob,

the father, with at least three feet of comforter
exclusive of the fringe hanging down before
him, and his threadbare clothes darned up and
brushed to look seasonable, and Tiny Tim upon
his shoulder. Alas for Tiny Tim, he bore a little
crutch, and had his limbs supported by an iron
frame !

"Why, where's our Martha?" cried Bob
Cratchit, looking round.

"Not coming," said Mrs. Cratchit.

"Not coming !" said Bob, with a sudden de-
clension in his high spirits ; for he had been
Tim's blood horse all the way from church, and
had come home rampant. "Not coming upon
Christmas Day !"

Martha did n't like to see him disappointed,
if it were only a joke ; so she came out prema-
turely from behind the closet door, and ran into
his arms, while the two young Cratchits hustled
Tiny Tim, and bore him off into the wash-house,
that he might hear the pudding singing in the
copper.

"And how did little Tim behave?" asked
Mrs. Cratchit, when she had rallied Bob on his
credulity, and Bob had hugged his daughter to
his heart's content.

"As good as gold," said Bob, "and better.

Somehow he gets thoughtful, sitting by himself
so much, and thinks the strangest things you
ever heard. He told me, coming home, that he
hoped the people saw him in the church, be-
cause he was a cripple, and it might be pleasant
to them to remember upon Christmas Day who
made lame beggars walk and blind men see."

Bob's voice was tremulous when he told them
this, and trembled more when he said that Tiny
Tim was growing strong and hearty.

His active little crutch was heard upon the
floor, and back came Tiny Tim before another
word was spoken, escorted by his brother and
sister to his stool beside the fire ; and while Bob,
turning up his cuffs, — as if, poor fellow, they
were capable of being made more shabby, —
compounded some hot mixture in a jug with gin
and lemons, and stirred it round and round and
put it on the hob to simmer, Master Peter and
the two ubiquitous young Cratchits went to fetch
the goose, with which they soon returned in high
procession.

Such a bustle ensued that you might have
thought a goose the rarest of all birds, — a feath-
ered phenomenon, to which a black swan was a
matter of course ; and in truth it was something
very like it in that house. Mrs. Cratchit made

the gravy (ready beforehand in a little saucepan)
hissing hot; Master Peter mashed the potatoes
with incredible vigor; Miss Belinda sweetened
up the apple-sauce; Martha dusted the hot
plates; Bob took Tiny Tim beside him in a tiny
corner at the table; the two young Cratchits set
chairs for everybody, not forgetting themselves,
and mounting guard upon their posts, crammed
spoons into their mouths, lest they should shriek
for goose before their turn came to be helped.
At last the dishes were set on, and grace was
said. It was succeeded by a breathless pause,
as Mrs. Cratchit, looking slowly all along the
carving-knife, prepared to plunge it in the breast;
but when she did, and when the long-expected
gush of stuffing issued forth, one murmur of delight arose all round the board, and even Tiny
Tim, excited by the two young Cratchits, beat
on the table with the handle of his knife, and
feebly cried Hurrah!

There never was such a goose. Bob said he
did n't believe there ever was such a goose
cooked. Its tenderness and flavor, size and
cheapness, were the themes of universal admi-
ration. Eked out by apple-sauce and mashed
potatoes, it was a sufficient dinner for the whole
family; indeed, as Mrs. Cratchit said with great

delight (surveying one small atom of a bone
upon the dish), they had n't ate it all at last!
Yet every one had had enough, and the young-
est Cratchits in particular were steeped in sage
and onion to the eyebrows! But now the plates
being changed by Miss Belinda, Mrs. Cratchit left
the room alone — too nervous to bear witnesses —
to take the pudding up, and bring it in.

Suppose it should not be done enough! Suppose it should break in turning out! Suppose
somebody should have got over the wall of the
back yard, and stolen it, while they were merry
with the goose, — a supposition at which the
two young Cratchits became livid! All sorts of
horrors were supposed.

Hallo! A great deal of steam! The pudding
was out of the copper. A smell like a washing-
day! That was the cloth. A smell like an eat-
ing-house and a pastry-cook's next door to each
other, with a laundress's next door to that!
That was the pudding! In half a minute Mrs.
Cratchit entered — flushed, but smiling proudly
— with the pudding, like a speckled cannon-ball,
so hard and firm, blazing in half of half-a-
quartern of ignited brandy, and bedight with
Christmas holly stuck into the top.

Oh, a wonderful pudding! Bob Cratchit said,

and calmly too, that he regarded it as the great-
est success achieved by Mrs. Cratchit since their
marriage. Mrs. Cratchit said that now the weight
was off her mind, she would confess she had her
doubts about the quantity of flour. Everybody
had something to say about it, but nobody said
or thought it was at all a small pudding for a
large family. It would have been flat heresy to
do so. Any Cratchit would have blushed to hint
at such a thing.

At last the dinner was all done, the cloth was
cleared, the hearth swept, and the fire made up.
The compound in the jug being tasted, and con-
sidered perfect, apples and oranges were put
upon the table, and a shovelful of chestnuts on
the fire. Then all the Cratchit family drew
round the hearth, in what Bob Cratchit called a
circle, meaning half a one ; and at Bob Cratchit's
elbow stood the family display of glass, — two
tumblers and a custard-cup without a handle.

These held the hot stuff from the jug, however, as well as golden goblets would have done ;
and Bob served it out with beaming looks, while
the chestnuts on the fire sputtered and cracked
noisily. Then Bob proposed : —

"A merry Christmas to us all, my dears. God
bless us."

Which all the family re-echoed.

"God bless us every one!" said Tiny Tim, the last of all.

He sat very close to his father's side, upon his little stool. Bob held his withered little hand in his, as if he loved the child, and wished to keep him by his side, and dreaded that he might be taken from him.

"Mr. Scrooge!" said Bob; "I'll give you, Mr. Scrooge, the Founder of the Feast!"

"The Founder of the Feast indeed!" cried Mrs. Cratchit, reddening. "I wished I had him here. I'd give him a piece of my mind to feast upon, and I hope he'd have a good appetite for it."

"My dear," said Bob, "the children! Christmas Day!"

"It should be Christmas Day, I am sure," said she, "on which one drinks the health of such an odious, stingy, hard, unfeeling man as Mr. Scrooge. You know he is, Robert! Nobody knows it better than you do, poor fellow!"

"My dear," was Bob's mild answer, "Christmas Day!"

"I'll drink his health for your sake and the Day's," said Mrs. Cratchit, "not for his. Long life to him! A merry Christmas and a happy

new year! He'll be very merry and very happy,
I have no doubt!"

The children drank the toast after her.  It
was the first of their proceedings which had no
heartiness in it!  Tiny Tim drank it last of all,
but he did n't care twopence for it.  Scrooge was
the Ogre of the family.  The mention of his
name cast a dark shadow on the party, which
was not dispelled for full five minutes.

After it had passed away, they were ten times
merrier than before, from the mere relief of
Scrooge the Baleful being done with.  Bob
Cratchit told them how he had a situation in
his eye for Master Peter, which would bring in,
if obtained, full five-and-sixpence weekly.  The
two young Cratchits laughed tremendously at the
idea of Peter's being a man of business; and
Peter himself looked thoughtfully at the fire from
between his collars, as if he were deliberating
what particular investments he should favor when
he came into the receipt of that bewildering in-
come.  Martha, who was a poor apprentice at a
milliner's, then told them what kind of work she
had to do, and how many hours she worked at
a stretch, and how she meant to lie abed to-
morrow morning for a good long rest; to-morrow
being a holiday she passed at home.  Also how

she had seen a countess and a lord some days
before, and how the lord "was much about as
tall as Peter," at which Peter pulled up his collars so high that you could n't have seen his
head if you had been there. All this time the
chestnuts and the jug went round and round;
and by and by they had a song, about a lost
child travelling in the snow, from Tiny Tim, who
had a plaintive little voice, and sang it very well
indeed.

*By Hans Christian Andersen.*

## CHRISTMAS CAROL.

CHILD Jesus comes from heavenly height,
    To save us from sin's keeping :
On manger straw, in darksome night,
    The Blessed One lies sleeping.
The star smiles down, the angels greet,
The oxen kiss the Baby's feet.
        Hallelujah, hallelujah,
            Child Jesus.

Take courage, soul, in grief cast down,
    Forget the bitter dealing :
A Child is born in David's town,
    To touch all souls with healing.
Then let us go and seek the Child,
Children like him, meek, undefiled.
        Hallelujah, hallelujah,
            Child Jesus.

*Anonymous.*

## LAST NIGHT, AS I LAY SLEEPING.

L AST night, as I lay sleeping,
  When all my prayers were said,
With my guardian angel keeping
  His watch above my head,
I heard his sweet voice carolling,
  Full softly on my ear,
A song for Christian boys to sing,
  For Christian men to hear:

" Thy body be at rest, dear boy,
  Thy soul be free from sin ;
I 'll shield thee from the world's annoy,
  And breathe pure words within.
The holy Christmas-tide is nigh,
  The season of Christ's birth ;
Glory be to God on high,
  And peace to men on earth.

" Myself and all the heavenly host
  Were keeping watch of old,

And saw the shepherds at their posts,
　　And all the sheep in fold.
Then told we, with a joyful cry,
　　The tidings of Christ's birth ;
Glory be to God on high,
　　And peace to men on earth.

" He bowed to all his Father's will,
　　And meek he was and lowly ;
And year by year his thoughts were still
　　Most innocent and holy.
He did not come to strive or cry,
　　But ever, from his birth,·
Gave glory unto God on high,
　　And peace to men on earth.

" Like him be true, like him be pure,
　　Like him be full of love ;
Seek not thine own, and so secure
　　Thine own that is above.
And still, as Christmas-tide draws nigh,
　　Sing thou of Jesus' birth ;
Glory be to God on high,
　　And peace to men on earth."

*By Charles Dickens.*

## CHRISTMAS DAY IN LONDON.

THE poulterers' shops were still half open, and the fruiterers' shops were radiant in their glory. There were great round, pot-bellied baskets of chestnuts, shaped like the waistcoats of jolly old gentlemen, lolling at the doors, and tumbling out into the street in their apoplectic opulence. There were ruddy, brown-faced, broad-girthed Spanish onions, shining in the fatness of their growth like Spanish Friars, and winking from their shelves in wanton slyness at the girls as they went by and glanced demurely at the hung-up mistletoe. There were pears and apples, clustered high in blooming pyramids ; there were bunches of grapes, made, in the shopkeepers' benevolence, to dangle from conspicuous hooks that people's mouths might water gratis as they passed ; there were piles of filberts, mossy and brown, recalling, in their fragrance, ancient walks among the woods, and pleasant

4

shufflings ankle-deep through withered leaves; there were Norfolk Biffins, squab and swarthy, setting off the yellow of the oranges and lemons, and, in the great compactness of their juicy persons, urgently entreating and beseeching to be carried home in paper bags and eaten after dinner. The very gold and silver fish, set forth among these choice fruits in a bowl, though members of a dull and stagnant-blooded race, appeared to know that there was something going on; and, to a fish, went gasping round and round their little world in slow and passionless excitement.

The Grocers'! oh, the Grocers'! nearly closed, with perhaps two shutters down, or one; but through those gaps such glimpses! It was not alone that the scales descending on the counter made a merry sound, or that the twine and roller parted company so briskly, or that the canisters were rattled up and down like juggling tricks, or even that the blended scents of tea and coffee were so grateful to the nose, or even that the raisins were so plentiful and rare, the almonds so extremely white, the sticks of cinnamon so long and straight, the other spices so delicious, the candied fruits so caked and spotted with molten sugar as to make the coldest lookers-on feel faint

IN THE CHURCH.

and subsequently bilious. Nor was it that the
figs were moist and pulpy, or that the French
plums blushed in modest tartness from their
highly decorated boxes, or that everything was
good to eat and in its Christmas dress; but the
customers were all so hurried and so eager in the
hopeful promise of the day, that they tumbled
up against each other at the door, crashing their
wicker baskets wildly, and left their purchases
upon the counter, and came running back to
fetch them, and committed hundreds of the like
mistakes, in the best humor possible; while the
Grocer and his people were so frank and fresh
that the polished hearts with which they fastened
their aprons behind might have been their own,
worn outside for general inspection, and for
Christmas daws to peck at if they chose.

But soon the steeples called good people all
to church and chapel; and away they came,
flocking through the streets in their best clothes
and with their gayest faces. And at the same
time there emerged from scores of by-streets,
lanes, and nameless turnings, innumerable people, carrying their dinners to the bakers' shops.
The sight of these poor revellers appeared to
interest the Spirit very much; for he stood with
Scrooge beside him in a baker's doorway, and

taking off the covers as their bearers passed, sprinkled incense on their dinners from his torch. And it was a very uncommon kind of torch; for once or twice when there were angry words between some dinner-carriers who had jostled each other, he shed a few drops of water on them from it, and their good humor was restored directly. For they said, it was a shame to quarrel upon Christmas Day. And so it was! God love it, so it was!

*By Charles Mackay.*

## UNDER THE HOLLY-BOUGH.

YE who have scorned each other,
    Or injured friend or brother,
  In this fast-fading year ;
Ye who, by word or deed,
Have made a kind heart bleed, —
    Come gather here.
Let sinned against and sinning
Forget their strife's beginning,
    And join in friendship now ;
Be links no longer broken,
Be sweet forgiveness spoken
    Under the holly-bough.

Ye who have loved each other,
Sister and friend and brother,
    In this fast-fading year ;
Mother and sire and child,
Young man and maiden mild, —
    Come gather here ;

And let your hearts grow fonder,
As memory shall ponder
    Each past unbroken vow :
Old loves and younger wooing
Are sweet in the renewing
    Under the holly-bough.


Ye who have nourished sadness,
Estranged from hope and gladness,
    In this fast-fading year ;
Ye with o'erburdened mind
Made aliens from your kind, —
    Come gather here.
Let not the useless sorrow
Pursue you night and morrow ;
    If e'er you hoped, hope now, —
Take heart, uncloud your faces,
And join in our embraces
    Under the holly-bough.

*By Hans Christian Andersen.*

## THE LITTLE MATCH-GIRL.

IT was terribly cold; it snowed and was already almost dark, and evening came on, — the last evening of the year. In the cold and gloom a poor little girl, bareheaded and barefoot, was walking through the streets. When she left her own house she certainly had had slippers on; but of what use were they? They were very big slippers, and her mother had used them till then, so big were they. The little maid lost them as she slipped across the road, where two carriages were rattling by terribly fast. One slipper was not to be found again; and a boy had seized the other, and run away with it. He thought he could use it very well as a cradle, some day when he had children of his own. So now the little girl went with her little naked feet, which were quite red and blue with the cold. In an old apron she carried a number of matches and a bundle of them in her hand. No one had bought anything of her all day, and no one had given her a farthing.

Shivering with cold and hunger, she crept along, a picture of misery, poor little girl ! The snowflakes covered her long fair hair, which fell in pretty curls over her neck ; but she did not think of that now. In all the windows lights were shining, and there was a glorious smell of roast goose, for it was New Year's Eve. Yes, she thought of that !

In a corner formed by two houses, one of which projected beyond the other, she sat down, cowering. She had drawn up her little feet, but she was still colder, and she did not dare to go home, for she had sold no matches, and did not bring a farthing of money. From her father she would certainly receive a beating ; and, besides, it was cold at home, for they had nothing over them but a roof through which the wind whistled, though the largest rents had been stopped with straw and rags.

Her little hands were almost benumbed with the cold. Ah ! a match might do her good, if she could only draw one from the bundle, and rub it against the wall, and warm her hands at it. She drew one out. R-r-atch ! how it sputtered and burned !  It was a warm bright flame, like a

little candle, when she held her hands over it ; it
was a wonderful little light ! It really seemed to
the little girl as if she sat before a great polished
stove, with bright brass feet and a brass cover.
How the fire burned ! how comfortable it was !
but the little flame went out, the stove vanished,
and she had only the remains of the burned
match in her hand.

A second was rubbed against the wall. It
burned up ; and when the light fell upon the wall
it became transparent like a thin veil, and she
could see through it into the room. On the
table a snow-white cloth was spread ; upon it
stood a shining dinner service ; the roast goose
smoked gloriously, stuffed with apples and dried
plums. And what was still more splendid to be-
hold, the goose hopped down from the dish, and
waddled along the floor, with a knife and fork in
its breast, to the little girl. Then the match
went out, and only the thick, damp, cold wall
was before her. She lighted another match.
Then she was sitting under a beautiful Christmas
tree ; it was greater and more ornamented than
the one she had seen through the glass door
at the rich merchant's. Thousands of candles
burned upon the green branches, and colored
pictures like those in the print shops looked

down upon them. The little girl stretched forth
her hand toward them; then the match went
out. The Christmas lights mounted higher.
She saw them now as stars in the sky: one of
them fell down, forming a long line of fire.

"Now some one is dying," thought the little
girl; for her old grandmother, the only person
who had loved her, and who was now dead, had
told her that when a star fell down a soul
mounted up to God.

She rubbed another match against the wall; it
became bright again, and in the brightness the
old grandmother stood clear and shining, mild
and lovely.

"Grandmother!" cried the child, "oh, take
me with you! I know you will go when the
match is burned out. You will vanish like the
warm fire, the warm food, and the great, glorious
Christmas tree!"

And she hastily rubbed the whole bundle of
matches, for she wished to hold her grandmother
fast. And the matches burned with such a glow
that it became brighter than in the middle of the
day; grandmother had never been so large or so
beautiful. She took the little girl in her arms,
and both flew in brightness and joy above the
earth, very, very high; and up there was neither

cold nor hunger nor care, — they were with God.

But in the corner, leaning against the wall, sat the poor girl with red cheeks and smiling mouth, frozen to death on the last evening of the Old Year. The New Year's sun rose upon a little corpse ! The child sat there, stiff and cold, with the matches, of which one bundle was burned. " She wanted to warm herself," the people said. No one imagined what a beautiful thing she had seen, and in what glory she had gone in with her grandmother to the New Year's Day.

*From George Wither's " Hallelujah."*

## A ROCKING HYMN.

SWEET baby, sleep ; what ails my dear?
　　What ails my darling thus to cry?
Be still, my child, and lend thine ear
　　To hear me sing thy lullaby.
　　　　　*My pretty lamb, forbear to weep ;*
　　　　　*Be still, my dear ; sweet baby, sleep.*


Thou blessed soul, what canst thou fear?
　　What thing to thee can mischief do?
Thy God is now thy Father dear ;
　　His holy Spouse thy Mother too.
　　　　　*Sweet baby, then, forbear to weep ;*
　　　　　*Be still, my babe ; sweet baby, sleep.*

.　　.　　.　　.　　.　　.　　.　　.　　.

Whilst thus thy lullaby I sing,
　　For thee great blessings ripening be ;
Thine eldest brother is a king,
　　And hath a kingdom bought for thee.
　　　　　*Sweet baby, then, forbear to weep ;*
　　　　　*Be still, my babe ; sweet baby, sleep.*

Sweet baby, sleep, and nothing fear ;
  For whosoever thee offends,
By thy protector threatened are,
  And God and angels are thy friends.
      *Sweet baby, then, forbear to weep ;*
      *Be still, my babe ; sweet baby, sleep.*

When God with us was dwelling here,
  In little babes he took delight :
Such innocents as thou, my dear,
  Are ever precious in his sight.
      *Sweet baby, then, forbear to weep ;*
      *Be still, my babe ; sweet baby, sleep.*

A little infant once was he,
  And Strength-in-Weakness then was laid
Upon his Virgin-Mother's knee,
  That power to thee might be conveyed.
      *Sweet baby, then, forbear to weep ;*
      *Be still, my babe ; sweet baby, sleep.*

In this thy frailty and thy need
  He friends and helpers doth prepare,
Which thee shall cherish, clothe, and feed,
  For of thy weal they tender are.
      *Sweet baby, then, forbear to weep ;*
      *Be still, my babe ; sweet baby, sleep.*

The King of kings, when he was born,
  Had not so much for outward ease ;
By him such dressings were not worn,
  Nor such-like swaddling-clothes as these.
      *Sweet baby, then, forbear to weep ;*
      *Be still, my babe ; sweet baby, sleep.*

Within a manger lodged thy Lord,
  Where oxen lay and asses fed ;
Warm rooms we do to thee afford,
  An easy cradle or a bed.
      *Sweet baby, then, forbear to weep ;*
      *Be still, my babe ; sweet baby, sleep.*

The wants that he did then sustain
  Have purchased wealth, my babe, for thee,
And by his torments and his pain
  Thy rest and ease securèd be.
      *My baby, then, forbear to weep ;*
      *Be still, my babe ; sweet baby, sleep.*

Thou hast (yet more), to perfect this,
  A promise and an earnest got
Of gaining everlasting bliss,
  Though thou, my babe, perceiv'st it not.
      *Sweet baby, then, forbear to weep ;*
      *Be still, my babe ; sweet baby, sleep.*

By *Alfred, Lord Tennyson.*
(Cantos XXVIII., XXIX., XXX.)

## IN MEMORIAM.

THE time draws near the birth of Christ :
  The moon is hid ; the night is still ;
The Christmas bells from hill to hill
Answer each other in the mist.

Four voices of four hamlets round,
    From far and near, on mead and moor,
    Swell out and fail, as if a door
Were shut between me and the sound :

Each voice four changes on the wind,
    That now dilate, and now decrease,
    Peace and good will, good will and peace,
Peace and good will, to all mankind.

This year I slept and woke with pain,
    I almost wished no more to wake,
    And that my hold on life would break
Before I heard those bells again :

But they my troubled spirit rule,
    For they controlled me when a boy ;
    They bring me sorrow touched with joy,
The merry, merry bells of Yule.

    .    .    .    .    .    .    .    .    .

With such compelling cause to grieve
    As daily vexes household peace,
    And chains regret to his decease,
How dare we keep our Christmas Eve ;

Which brings no more a welcome guest
    To enrich the threshold of the night
    With showered largess of delight,
In dance and song and game and jest.

Yet go, and while the holly-boughs
    Entwine the cold baptismal font,
    Make one wreath more for Use and Wont,
That guard the portals of the house ;

Old sisters of a day gone by,
    Gray nurses, loving nothing new ;
    Why should they miss their yearly due
Before their time ?   They too will die.

With trembling fingers did we weave
 The holly round the Christmas hearth ;
 A rainy cloud possessed the earth,
And sadly fell our Christmas Eve.

At our old pastimes in the hall
 We gambolled, making vain pretence
 Of gladness, with an awful sense
Of one mute Shadow watching all.

We paused : the winds were in the beech :
 We heard them sweep the winter land ;
 And in a circle hand-in-hand
Sat silent, looking each at each.

Then echo-like our voices rang ;
 We sung, though every eye was dim,
 A merry song we sang with him
Last year : impetuously we sang :

We ceased : a gentler feeling crept
 Upon us : surely rest is meet :
 " They rest," we said, " their sleep is sweet,"
And silence followed, and we wept.

5

Our voices took a higher range ;
   Once more we sang : " They do not die,
   Nor lose their mortal sympathy,
Nor change to us, although they change :

" Rapt from the fickle and the frail
   With gathered power, yet the same,
   Pierces the keen seraphic flame
From orb to orb, from veil to veil."

Rise, happy morn, rise, holy morn,
   Draw forth the cheerful day from night :
   O Father, touch the east, and light
The light that shone when Hope was born.